LOVE LOST

A NEON SUNRISE ANTHOLOGY

Introduction

I can hear you now — "Love? Really? Are you that cliché?" I get it. As someone who identifies as a poet and has written pages of verse on the subject, I can see why you might be thinking that I've chosen to wander down the easy path with this volume. And you might be right. You might also need to take a few steps back and consider your viewpoint on the material might be a bit narrow.

"Love is a many splendored thing," or so we've been told. It's all we need and it makes the world go round. You can fall into it — or out of it — but it's ultimately something you choose to do. Love is complicated. Doesn't matter if it's romantic, platonic, familial or something else — there's typically far more going on than is immediately apparent. It's multi-faceted and mysterious and several other adjectives that might spice things up.

When it came to deciding the next thematically based anthology for Neon Sunrise, love was a bit of an obvious choice. I'm not one for making things one-sided though, so the experience of "love" was left open to a wide interpretation. People react to a range of ideas and emotions tied to love in their lives and I wanted this book to reflect the depth of that range as much as possible.

12 authors from across the globe answered the call for submissions and each brought their own individual experience to these pages. There is romance, heartbreak, infatuation, loss, desire, contentment, and so much more. Through it all, the constant is love and our human expression.

We hope you find something that resonates within these pages and that our words strike a chord. Love is indeed a subject full of mystery and wonder, and we hope that carries you through the moments of pain and loss that are often close behind. In the end the love is always worth it.

See you where the sidewalk ends,
David Greshel
June 2022

Acknowledgements

There are so many things that go into putting a book together. Neon Sunrise may be a one-person operation on paper, but none of this would be possible without the support of so many different people.

Thank you to friends and family for the encouragement and shared excitement to see this project come to life.

Thank you to everyone that supported the Kickstarter campaign and shared in the marketing and promotion.

Thank you Heidi, Stephanie, Heather, Jason, Sophia, Peter, Malika, Danielle, Dylan, Star, and Liz. for wanting to be a part of this project and for providing your amazing talent. This book doesn't exist without you, and I'm grateful that you've trusted me to bring your work to the world.

Thank you to Matt McKay for providing the original art used for the cover. I'm excited to see where your graphic design career takes you and I'm thankful for the years of friendship we've shared.

Additional Art Credits

Pg. 3 – Steve Zmijewski
Pg. 8 – Pete Linforth
Pg. 123 – Gordon Johnson

A special acknowledgement and an extra-sized thank you to all of the following people who helped bring this project to life on Kickstarter. Your sense of community and support is incredibly valuable and we could not have done this without you!

Travis Gibb
JonathanHedrickComics.com
Peter J. King
Davy Lee
Stephanie Guasp
You Rock Heidi!
Star Kaat
Danielle Montgomery
Joel Gonzalez
Leanne Kathleen Ingino
Nicole Widrig
Deb Walsh
Jennifer Knapp
Brian W
SC
TC
Christina Cardenas
Jonathan Mundell
Steve Zmijewski
S. R. Malone
Pete Riesett
Matt Kund
Rachel Mintz
Liz Lugo
Cliff Smithson
Bret Eayrs
Don Nguyen
Mary Berger
Rick Shea
Roselili Vargas
Kingdom of Comics
Finish Line Comics
Andew Abarca
Taurus Comics
Tom Sokolowski
Nancy Parker
Nicholas Stephenson

Zoe Kaplan
Joshua Dobbs
Chris Ballinger
Eron Wyngarde
Scott Schiffmacher
Thea Flurry
Joanne Williams
Rachel Carroll
Frontline Comics
Rebecca King

Heidi Hess

Longing

Claudia sat on the hardened piece of pleather that was supposed to be a school bus bench seat. In between watching the rain come down in long slow drips on the double-framed windows, she stared at her reflection. Was she sad? Maybe. Confused was more like it.

The bus grumbled with a start and then lurched forward pulling Claudia and the rest of her classmates away from Forge Hill High School. She pulled her legs up and wrapped her arms around them to comfort her while she replayed the events of the last twenty-four hours. She knew what she'd do when she got off the bus. Rain or not she was headed to Corey's house. She wanted answers.

He wasn't in school and she hadn't heard anything from him all day. Needless to say, she was slightly miffed. She sat in thought for the next ten minutes. If someone had told her that she was going to fall so hard for the new kid in such a short amount of time she would have told them they were crazy. Six months. Had it only been six months? Corey was from Portland. He stuck out like a sore thumb in New York. And even though he made friends easily he never changed who he was - plaid shirt, combat boots, jeans, and that smirk peeking out from under his dark bangs that were way too long. She loved **the** way his black glossy hair shimmered in the sunlight and the particular way he had of leaning on things... it exuded an easy confidence. At least that was the side he showed people. There were other things... more sensitive tender spots that he showed her when they were curled up staring at the stars in between chain-smoking cigarettes. And now - no show at school. No text. She wasn't mad... she was confused. What had happened?

"Are you serious?"

"Come on... I'm new here...this might be fun."

Claudia was standing on the steps. She reflexively put her hand on her hip, leaned to one side, and looked over the dark frame of her glasses giving Corey "The Eye". They were supposed to go out on a date and it was his turn to plan it but... a ghost tour? In her hometown? First of all, it sounded cheesy. Second, she knew Forge Hill like the back of her hand. The sightings in the cemetery? She knew about that. Mrs. Harris's three-story brownstone in town that was supposed to have a light in the attic window on certain nights? Yep. She actually saw that one. Oh wait, don't forget the abandoned farm just outside of town with the phantom cows that would cross the road. O.k., that one she hadn't seen but she knew about it. The point was that she already knew everything there was to know about Forge Hill. Corey climbed the steps. Looped his arm with hers, looked out at the street, and then back down at her. "Come on. We'll go and make fun of everything. Humor me." Claudia let out a long sigh and reluctantly breathed out "O.k...".

The tour itself was meeting about four blocks away in the touristy part of town. There was a small table outside of a gift shop. Its black table cloth had "Haunted Forge Hill" scrawled on it. The gentleman behind the table had on a long cloak and a dark tall hat reminiscent of the Victorian era. He was faking an accent and this whole thing made Claudia chuckle. She handed him their tickets while being nudged by Corey. It was the kind of nudge that said "Cut it out.." There were a few more people that trickled in and in just a few minutes this mock creepy dude was walking them through town pointing out the cemetery, having the others look for the light in Mrs. Harris's window, and even taking them to the edge of town to explain the phantom cow phenomenon. The entire time Claudia and Corey were arm in arm exchanging giggles. There was one last stop on the tour and they were surprised when it was right in front of Corey's house. The gentleman spoke "Now this house," the guide began "take a good look at all of the windows. It is said that over a hundred years ago a colony of bats took over the house. The family that lived there disappeared and were never heard from again. But to this day, in the early evening, you may see a few bats coming out of the attic rafters and taking to the night sky." Claudia cleared her throat. "Umm. excuse me, sir." The guide took his gaze off of the top windows that he had been studying and turned his attention to the couple. Corey was embarrassed, to say the least. No one could see his cheeks glowing crimson in the dark. Claudia continued "I know the family that lives here. There are no bats. They have never noticed anything unusual." The guide returned his gaze to the rest of the group and then back to the house. "That's the beauty of a good ghost story; Some of it is real, some of it is folklore. But what matters is what you want to believe." Claudia and Corey exchanged a look as the tour guide finished his tour. Everyone was dismissed. Even though they were in front of Corey's house there was no way he was letting her walk home alone in the dark.

The night air was thick and misty. They decided to take the long way home as they relished the feel of their hands intertwined. Now and then they took a few minutes to stop and kiss. Claudia couldn't help but feel like kissing Corey was similar to being kissed by a butterfly - light, soft, almost fluttery kisses. Most of the boys that had come before were clumsy and oafish on their best nights. Corey was different.

On the steps, he held her hand and kissed it. Then he bent to kiss her forehead, then her nose, and finally her lips. He pulled back, looked her in the eyes, and whispered "Good night, sweet angel." He watched her walk up the rest of the steps. She turned, looked at him, sighed, and gave him a small wave before going inside. He was a dream.

Claudia slung her backpack on and hopped off the last step of the bus. It was still raining but she didn't care. She headed up the street to Corey's house and after about half a block the rain was coming down so hard it was running down her face. She stopped, wiped her glasses with a part of her t-shirt that was still dry. The water just smeared around on the lenses. She threw them back on. It was better than having no glasses. His house was just around the corner and as she turned the bend she could feel that something was not right. It was way too quiet. The windows of the other houses looked down on her. She felt as if she were being watched. And Claudia wasn't sure, maybe it was the rain, but the browns and grays of the buildings and streets seemed darker... almost sinister. There was his house. It was just two doors down now. Corey would clear this up... this would all make sense.

She stood at the bottom of the steps and looked up. The house was dark and void of activity. She pressed on taking the steps two at a time. She used the knocker. A hollow "knock, knock" came from the other side of the door. She opened it and peeked around. The house was dark and empty. Her first thoughts were "Wait - what?" She quickly closed the door and backed up. She lost her footing and stumbled back a few steps on the stairs only to land on her backpack on the sidewalk. Rain poured on her face as she stared up and tried to make sense of what had just happened. Where the hell was Corey? She got to her feet and considered that maybe she had the wrong house. Her glasses were blurry. Yes, surely that was it. But she looked harder and the number 14 was right there above the door. The way it had always been. She scratched her head and started up the street slowly trying to figure out what to do next.

The table was set up in the same spot as last night and the same gentleman was there. Claudia approached the table. Based on his reaction she must have been a sight. "Well.." He stepped back a little "Hello there. Back for more?" He inquired. "No... listen..." She began "the tour last night... the guy with me... you stopped in front of his house. His family is the one living there...and now they are gone." Claudia trailed off. Putting words to the reality of the situation put hairline cracks in her heart. She could feel something draining out. "I remember you," the tour guide said cautiously "but you were by yourself." Claudia's world was starting to spin. "No..." Claudia stammered "I gave you two tickets. We were holding hands...". She sat down right in front of the table completely dumbfounded. The tour guide came around the side of the table "I'm sorry but it was just you." His voice got soft "Hey, are you o.k.?" Claudia's hands reflexively went to her head and she started shaking uncontrollably. He approached her but she was up in a flash and took off down the street. She wasn't sure where she was going. All she knew was that she had to move. The hairline cracks were now bold fissures and whatever it was that was draining out was being replaced with emptiness. She found herself at the steps of his house again. And again went up the steps and pushed open the door. The interior was cold, dark, and damp. The emptiness of the room chilled her but it echoed what was in her heart now. She thought of all of the promises and memories. Tears popped up and she began to cry. The foyer was high and the staircase climbed the walls up to the third floor. Light filtered in from above through the glass ceiling. Claudia stared up and cried and was surprised to find there was rage building inside her. It worked its way up until she was screaming at the top of her lungs. She closed her tear-stained eyes and surrendered to it. Her screams echoed throughout the house and rattled the windows. After her screams subsided, there in the quiet recesses of the house she could hear a small ruffling. It grew a bit louder and then down the stairs came a black cloud. Claudia turned to leave but this cloud surrounded her. A swarm of bats was circling her, pulling at her hair, clothes, and backpack. There were so many that it blocked out her vision but they appeared to be creating a face... it was Corey. Her beloved's face was being created by this cloud of bats flying around her. The soft fluttering of bat wings seemed to have him say something... what was he saying? She reached out to touch what would have been his face. The noise from the bats was creating a whisper of a voice. "Goodbye sweet angel." Fresh tears were upon her now. "Goodbye..." She whispered. The large cracks in her heart grew deeper and she fell to her knees, unable to withstand the pain. And just as quickly as the bats had descended upon her, they were gone. Corey was gone. What was left of her heart was gone and in those large open spaces where love had once lived there grew something else... something that would stay with her the rest of her life - it was longing.

Heidi Hess is a writer and artist living the good life in Lake Worth, FL. Her curious mind and vivid imagination lends itself to writing stories like Chasing Elpis, poems and comic scripts. At any given time she can be found peeking around the next corner with her two kids, Savannah and Ryan looking for their next adventure. Or coffee cup in hand, yoga pants, messy hair feverishly typing out her next new world. She is very excited to be included in A Light That Never Goes Out and would love to hear your feedback.

Check out her social media to stay in touch:
Facebook: Heidi Hess
Twitter: @CreatesHeidi
Instagram: @createsheidi
Email: hhess82@gmail.com

Stephanie Guasp

-Tide

I've had a poem lodged in the back of my throat for you
For what feels like eternity
Never the right words for you
I sputter and choke on the yoke of you
But this load is too heavy to drag
So it lives in the tree of me
Tangled in my roots, I use my tongue to get free of me
The grass that called to you was much greener
Like the other side of the fence had emeralds for eyes
Jade surprise
You know, I never cried for you
Afraid I'd call oceans into existence
Drown the world as we know it
Instead, I bide my time for a time that's right
For a word that could somehow pull into sight
The magnitude of losing a moon
And what it does to the tide

-Philomena

My grandmother was a tree.
I would climb her knotted, twisted joints to sit in the palm of her branches
I could listen to her leaves rustle all day
The wisdom of her crown brushing the sky
Her roots ran deep, she was unshakable
And her bark was worse than her bite
Her sap was as sweet as maple
And she shared it with anyone under her shade
Sure, she lost her foliage in the winter
But come spring, she'd be in full bloom
Philomena was a tree.
She taught me to stand still even in the strongest wind
She taught me to bury myself in the soil of life
And that if I kept at it, I would one day blossom

- The Cursive of Stars

The sky was alight with levitating gems
Diamonds we could seemingly pluck for our pockets
Instead, we left them there as talisman
Guarding our secrets
Watching over us as we parted with our laughter
With reckless abandon
We would invent constellations
Write our opus in the cursive of stars
The wind was our sentinel
Carrying our joys and fears on its breeze
The ocean was our choir
The crashing waves a symphony
Us, their captive audience
Bathed in the moonlight, we puffed dreams like cigarettes
Taking turns filling the air with soliloquy
We were alone, together
Truth be told, I'd never felt better
Than when our toes were in the sand
And our heads were in the clouds
Reaching for the breath of God

-Spare

O bitter, blanketed, blackened stars-
Frigid, forlorn, and charred despite
The icy cold- subsumed by night...

O burning ball of
Noxious fire
Writhing beneath a halo
Of poisoned light

Kiss me like Icarus,
Hungry for the burning bliss,
The blaze of the sun's tongue,
Kiss me so I, too, can sleep
With a mouthful of salt-
No more time to keep...

If it means soaring high
Rather than remaining
Etherized upon your table
If you're able,
That is...
To spare a kiss
In times like these-
I'd cherish to be free.

Stephanie has been reading and writing poetry as far back as she can remember. From Shel Silverstein to Kahlil Gibran and everyone between, her thirst for beautiful language is insatiable. When she's not writing poetry, Stephanie enjoys penning lyrics and making music. She's also an avid gamer and doting dog mom to her 10-year-old lab mix, Bodhi. She's passionate about travel and can't wait to get back to Europe when the time is right. You can follow her for writing and photography on Instagram: @sguasp or check out her music on YouTube, channel name sguasp27.

Jason Lee

So you've decided to read a book on love? For that I applaud you.
While Love is a theme I have found, sometimes despite my best efforts to the contrary, has often influenced my writing, it has rarely been amongst the art which I've been led to share, for one reason or another.
Previously, I will admit, I suspected precious few would be able to appreciate the way in which I wrote on the subject. At this juncture, I barely care.

Thus, it was with some great satisfaction that I submitted to this collection a few of my works that might well have otherwise continued to languish in obscurity.

So, to those who welcome and celebrate this theme, in all it's bitter and sweet, highs and lows, to you go my utmost respect, gratitude and yes, love as well..

Ardor

How do I love words?
Let me count the ways

I love them
In perfect prosaic symmetry
breathtaking in beauty,

In soaring arias of the ecstatic
taken flight,

In quavering quorums of grief
beyond consolation,

In roaring declarations
of triumphant defiance!...

And in the luminous stillness
of reflection given shape

I love them,
As I love you:
Your face,
Your hands,
Your voice,
Your heart

Kitsuge

It was broken that day

And when it did
Break,
It shattered into what seemed like
a million pieces,
fragments scattered so far
Strewn like the glittering stars,
I still don't know if I'll ever find them again

I thought we could
mend it,
piece it back together,
...together
"together"
Even that word
seemed like a foreign concept to you

The gravity of your impropriety
fused with your disdain for my pain
Creating a bludgeoning force

Intent on dismantling my moment of decision
Designed to destroy all vestige of resolve
for the battles ahead,

Another little death
Among so many

Another sorrow among sorrows

One I fear,
you'll never understand
So what have I to do
but begin again?

Vessels

1.

When I touch her
Hold her
My senses grieve
Her longing

A silent
Unvoiced prayer:

Cling to me
Desperately
Cling to me
Like ivy

Lover

Break into
My private prison;
Your fearless want
Shattering,
Your love
Sundering

Till I'm shuddered open
Rendered beautifully broken

All prisoners
No longer
Held
Within

Incarceration
Sentences,
Terms,
Ended

Forever

2.

Can my desire
Equate
Your ennui?

Can my longing
Surmount
Your sorrow?

Wounded
Wilting
Like past prime
Lilly

Awaiting the rains
You whither
In vain:

The well availing,
I draw forth
Your need

Missing

I miss,
The way I never saw
you walk,
run your fingers
through your wind blown
Hair

Your skin glowing
beneath the
streaming rays,
The color of
stained glass

I miss,
never seeing
Your smile spread
across your lips,
Your eyes lit
with mirth
and gratitude

Never yet had
the pleasure
to watch you
cry
To feel your
heartbeat
echo my own

To choose presence
To know regret
To hope for
new tomorrows...

How do you miss
the things you never knew?

Yet, somehow
I do
I miss you

Red Queen

You would make
me, eternal
petitioner

Persimmon sweet,
feigning sincerity
from your
crumbling throne:
Lofty these
lowly heights

My heartfelt concessions, fuel
for your egocentric
machinations
offerings consumed
in the hungry brazen flames

A duty
too many
adore
in your "Have Not" kingdom

My affections
    Even love
Deemed contraband
to be expunged

For there is no having
Here,
No holding...
Only wanting
Ever
    Wanting

 Jason Lee is a naturalized Floridian and long-time poet, hailing originally from PA and currently residing in the Space Coast. Having originally taken up writing poetry as a way of coping with the challenges of young adulthood, only in the last decade, thanks to a variety of inspiring artists and friends throughout his life, has he had the vision and desire to find his voice in verse, publish, or perform his art publicly. Even so, it was not until after 2014, when he suffered a tragic and unexpected loss, that this endeavor began in earnest.

In total, he's been published six times, appearing in four anthologies, as well as two poetry collections of his own work. He is presently working on a third collection which is slated for release by or before the fall of 2022. He has shared his writing many times in various venues and formats including Slam competition and enjoys the challenge of poetry being transmuted when taken from one medium to another.

While Jason enjoys both writing and editing, he also is a purveyor of a wide variety of the arts beyond the literary. He particularly relishes the finer things in life, including, but not limited to, food and wine.
He aspires to share and utilize his talents, experiences, and appreciations on a wider scale in the future and is open to connecting and collaborating with other like-minded artists.

You can find him on Facebook and Instagram
@TheHarbingerSpeaks

"Prate not to me of suicide, Faint heart in battle, not for pride I say Endure, but that such end denied Makes welcomer yet the death that's to be died."
— Stevie Smith

Liz Lugo

Can you remember the taste
of my lips in your dreams?
Your arms around my waist.
Your gaze intertwined mine, a gleam.

So close, I could hear your silence.
So close, I remained silent.
Your breath near my cheek.
I begged to God in your chest to sleep.

A kiss.
At that moment,
all I wanted.

Can you remember that time
(in your dream)
I stole every corner of your mind;
killed you with caresses and kisses,
what a beautiful crime!

So close, my heart melted.
So close, your heart fused.
Shyness, passionate daydream.
Denying it, an awful sin.

To be in the place
only in dreams
I've been... your arms.

Can you remember how we smiled?
A whisper, our souls bristled; desire.
In your dreams, peaceful and wild.
Kiss me. I want to wake there; entire.

 Liz Lugo is a Puerto Rican self-published poet with a bachelor's degree in Microbiology. Following her passion for cinema, she pursued a certification in Professional Screenwriting from UCLA School of Theater, Film, and Television. She later partook in a TV writing workshop with writer and producer Gloria Calderon-Kellet. Liz recently obtained her MFA in Professional Screenwriting.

As a part of a class project, she wrote and directed a supernatural horror short film titled "Lamentos del Silencio." In 2019, she worked as a Script Supervisor in "Don't Blink." Later in 2020, Liz won the Grand Prize at the Various Artists independent Film Festival for her work as a writer/director in Run. Hide. Pray., a proof-of-concept for one of her feature screenplays. This prize leads to the production of a music video directed by Liz.

Her upcoming short film is a psychological horror thriller titled "I Killed Lucy Jones." Her stories are mostly identified by inclusion and diversity, including Hispanics and Deaf characters, and situations that highlight at least one of the following causes she's committed to: verbal abuse, sexual abuse, rape, human rights, mental health, equality, among others. She works mostly with elements of horror, sci-fi, psychological thriller, and post-apocalyptic, and you will always find them linked to her Puerto Rican culture.

Liz also enjoys comedy, documentaries, westerns, foreign films, and has an extreme fascination for comics/graphic novels. When she's not writing or analyzing films or TV shows, she's up to a new adventure or just hearing music, dancing, cooking, or exercising.

"Dream the impossible and you'll get the unexpected." LL

Heather R. Parker

orbits: the beginning

this pull to you
(like the moon)
pushes and pulls the tide
the ebb and flow
pulling us into the earth
(like gravity)
we circle each other
a decadent dance
bound to each other
(like rhythmic orbits)
there we were
a piece of the same star
galaxies entwined
(in our eyes)
born of all the light
within you
within me

the light from moonbeams: ever closer

I feel you coming
it swells within me
(this essence of you)
the light from moonbeams
salt from the sea
(upon your fated lips)
the gravity of the earth
upon the most delicate
of butterfly wings
I feel you coming
(I feel you)
deep within
you: earth
me: sky
I will blanket you
in an ocean
(of stars)

a drift of stars: the collision

it was your music
that found me
those tiny pieces
(fragments)
scattered galaxies you found
and stitched back together
creating a heartsong
to scatter into
the space-sky
littered with the debris
of the faded
muted past
your heartsong
(drifting through the aether)
little birds
that fluttered into
my caged heart
now set free
my heart
follows your light
we collide
(softly)
you: a whisper
me: a glimmer
the wind blows
in my hair
tendrils of starlight
kissed by your fierce
storm petals
so fragrant
with your touch
a drift of stars
behind my eyes
you burn
ghosts on my eyelids
memories of you

steady earth: the dust settles

I am now:
still water
and fire moons
you:
turbulent ocean
and calm
steady earth
your waters
soothe my
frenzied
rough
edges
my fire is
your scorched earth
moon to moon
star to star
you pull me
ever closer

heart-sky: I am home

you encircle,
you enfold
our orbits
once distinct
now one synchronized
heartbeat
I am now:
home
in the galaxy
of your arms
you: my harbor of love
my love is the moon
barely contained
in my bleeding heart-sky

 Heather R. Parker is a freelance writer, editor, and poet from Georgia. Her work has been published by Synthetic Reality, Nightingale & Sparrow, Goats Milk, Analog Submissions Press, Between Shadows Press, Friday Flash Fiction, Clover & Be, 365 Tomorrows, Entropy Squared, and others. In her spare time, you can find her doing yoga, taking long walks in the woods, birdwatching, or picking flowers in sun-dappled meadows. You can follow her work on Instagram and Fictionate.Me.

Danielle Montgomery

Planting flowers on the other side of the world

I wonder how long the flowers lived
the ones I planted for you on top of Mount Whitfield
bright, violet pansies sprouting from dusty, arid earth
the same way your bright, vibrant soul radiated
from a withered body you refused to water
surviving solely off the fumes from
tacky hairspray and B&H Gold
it's a wonder you didn't succumb to the soil sooner
even your front tooth was uprooted
I remember how it would wobble when you'd talk
swaying in the breeze of your Tetley Tea breath
like a lonely, forgotten clothes peg
clinging to the washing line during a springtime storm
unabashedly frantic, inevitably broken
if you were a garden you'd have been overgrown
with branches of endless adventure
untame hair the texture of woodland bramble
cascaded wildly past the peaks of your shoulders
creases as deep as canyons scored your weathered face
their river beds planted with the fruits of accidental wisdom
that would bloom while tucking me in at night

nine years have passed since I planted those flowers
on a secluded mountain in tropical north Queensland
and I like to imagine they're still there
the same way I like to imagine you're still here
as stubborn as ivy and as resilient as cacti
whenever I close my eyes
I can see the sparkle in your crooked smile
and you're still breathing
                              you're still thriving.

Sleeping with ghosts

You can find me in the hollowed spaces
between our bed sheets
sallow skin flecked with goosebump armour
a held breath fighting against cold air
weighed down by the emptiness in my lungs
I'm left clutching at these magnolia prison walls
waiting for your touch to ripple through me
and absolve me of virtue
the same way the velvet midnight sky
penetrates the innocent horizon
sunlight reduced to a salacious secret
whispered between longing lips
        this is my death bed, darling
you can find me where our love perished

Love lost to time

I keep your love in an urn above the fireplace
and mourn the chances we didn't take
like learning how to waltz under summer's moonlight
or ravishing each other's bodies during a storm
a million moments, forever lost to the clock hand's grasp
haunt me when I hear the swoon of Sinatra
or feel thunder rumbling between my legs
I want to savour seconds the way you savoured chocolate
gently caressing it with your delectable tongue
as though you may never taste anything sweet again
I want to melt into the pores of your silky smooth skin
and keep my lips pressed against the bones in your chest
until I meet my fate and disintegrate into the sky
finding a cloud to call my home
                              but I can't make love to ghosts
so I'll quietly kiss the mosaic vase
that holds the remains of our memories
and hope you'll meet me in the watery depths
of my dreams where time   stands still.

Stale

Our love is like loose cheddar cheese
in a ziplock bag
questionable, infuriating
there's no reason for it but there it is
two cubes of mouldy milk
left to fester in a plastic cocoon
edges hardening, appeal diminishing
foul smells manifesting in the bedroom
      but it's salvageable if we act now
a rosemary cracker and the last dregs of wine
maybe even a grape or two on the side

that ought to do it
      we'll be just fine

Danielle Montgomery is from Birmingham, UK, where she's a copywriter and content manager by day, and part-time poet by night. Many moons ago, she blogged about mental health and also contributed to The Huffington Post, however writing poetry was always a personal endeavour. In 2019, she completed a poetry course in London led by acclaimed poet, Christina Dunhill, and a year later during lockdown, took the plunge to start sharing her poems with the world via Instagram (@danielle_emme_poetry). Although previously unpublished until now, she's hopeful this won't be the last you see of her.

Peter J. King

The Persistence of Memory

This cotton pillowcase conceals
a block of foam within a vinyl skin,
hard-wearing and robust.

Like granite worn away
by centuries of dripping rain,
the pillow has been penetrated,
permeated by your murmured name.

And those who sleep here after me
will find their dreams
are haunted, though they won't
know who you are.

Letter Writing

I sit and write in silence,
outwardly composed and calm;
my hand is steady,
and the pen moves back and forth
without a tremor.
Inside me, though, the lava roils
red hot and bubbling,
and I'm amazed
that ink and paper are unscorched,
that I can fold the pages,
slide them in an envelope,
and send them to you,
every word a burning kiss.

Separation

the months will flash by,
      so they tell me,
and before I know it
        I'll be back with you.

they're wrong, of course:
I'm back with you
     at every moment
        of the dragging days.

Apart

Because I'm here, and you so far away,
Each minute is an hour, each day a year.
Outside the grass is sere, the sky is grey,
Because I'm here.

As March moves on to April, then to May,
Spring does it's usual thing: the leaves appear,
The young are reared in nest and den and dray.

But I can find no pleasure in the play
Of sunlight through the trees, nor in the clear
Sweet song of goldfinch or the jeering jay,
Because I'm here.

<u>Conflagrations</u>

Water constitutes the bulk of living bodies,
    held, contained, and always aging.
Life is growing old — the drawing in
                                of oxygen,
    which burns, which wafts us closer
        to the little heat death that awaits us all.
Life is burning water.

                  *

Thought challenges our comprehension,
    constituting what we try to understand
        as well as what it is that does the trying.
Consciousness is bursting out,
                        a personal
    Big Bang, a supernova burning
        at the centre of our being.
Consciousness is burning thought.

                  *

Bridges carry one across the barriers
    that separate us each from each.
Love is knowing that,
                the barrier traversed,
    we cannot simply turn,
        retrace our steps.
Love is burning bridges.

Peter J. King was born and brought up in Boston, Lincolnshire. Active on the London poetry scene in the 1970s as writer, performer, publisher, and editor, he returned to poetry in 2013 after a long absence, and has since been widely published in magazines and anthologies, including Shoreline of Infinity, Penumbric, Eye to the Telescope, and Eccentric Orbits II (ed. Wendy Van Camp). He also translates poetry, mainly from modern Greek (with Andrea Christofidou) and German, writes short prose, and paints. His currently available collections are Adding Colours to the Chameleon (Wisdom's Bottom Press) and All What Larkin (Albion Beatnik Press).

https://wisdomsbottompress.wordpress.com/

A. Loxley

Thimble

She put her heart
In a thimble
He took and crushed it
Ever so nimble

She gave everything
And much more
He consumed it
And returned a bore

She gave her soul
With love and pleasure
He took from her a toll
With selfish ignorance

Upon The Rocks

There she was
upon the rocks
Dead she was
upon the rocks

Killed she was
upon the rocks
Dashed in anger
upon the rocks

There I found her
upon the rocks
Take me too
upon the rocks

Wading in
upon the rocks
Cradling her
upon the rocks

Tears fall
upon the rocks
My heart breaks
upon the rocks

At Night By The Sea

Take my hand
Hold me close
Warm to my cold
At night by the sea

Whisper to me
Above the waves
Of love and longing
At night by the sea

So soon?
You've but returned
To home, to me
At night by the sea

Please stay
I cannot be
Cold and alone
At night by the sea

Take My Colors

Take my colors
  sir knight
For you will be
  my champion

Wear them proudly
  upon your helm
Bear them secretly
  tucked against you

Come for me soon
  my love, my lord
Another seeks to be
  my love, my lord

Do you love me still
  dearest heart
What bars your way
  to mine own side

The enemy will wait
  no longer
By force, to church
  I am taken

In sorrow do I
  warm his bed
In pain do I
  bear his children

Do my ladies see
  my unshed tears
Does the court know
  the beauty hidden misery

Wait! Stop not the boy
    tattered, mute, messenger
Deeply with tears he bows
    forehead to floor

Holding, offering, gently
    in shrunken arms
Reaching, clutching, pale
    in shaking arms

A rag to most
    hues all faded
My heart stops
    stained light and dark

Take my colors
    sir knight
For you will be
    my champion

The Elven Maid

Sunlight glowed
On the elven maid
Trees leaned in
Toward the elven maid

Flowers swayed and danced
With the elven maid
Sweetest birds
Listened to the elven maid

With abandon
Danced the elven maid
In longing melody
Sang the elven maid

In love collapsed
For the elven maid
In hope cried out
To the elven maid

Clasped in twilit meadow
Hand of the elven maid
Gained through eternity
Heart of the elven maid

 A Loxley is happiest in a forest, and spends her days researching and daydreaming.

Malika Kahn

The Tiptoeing Dilemma

I had to tell a lie today
although I'm no keen liar.
Cornered to construct a tale
to dissuade a man's desire.

Uninterest is a wound to pride
and outright rejection is sin.
Tactful refusals never work if tried
so at the end of the day we
      just
          don't
             win.
Must a bruised ego and heavy heart
really bring civility to an end?
When a simple no becomes something hard
...no wonder lies replace what's truly meant.

Respectfully, No

I can't
That's it.
That's all I have to say.
Not sure why you'd expect this to go any other way.
Look.
A spiral.
Surrounding me completely.
It's called a boundary and it means leave me be.

Cautiously Optimistic

To love is to be vulnerable
—a terrifying endeavour,
unless the one who holds your heart
is not inclined to sever.

I'm told that's impossible to know
without taking a leap of faith.
But isn't there a way guarded souls can find love
and come out of it unscathed?

Or is that the point of it all—
to hold out your hand in the dark
hoping the hand that reaches for it
ignites a reassuring spark.

Like an arrow to the heart.
Guided.

Such is Love

eyes glisten as he ponders, slipping into a faraway stare
chiselled cheekbones, gentle soul, a transparency that is rare

the more I get to know him, the more undeserving I feel
sometimes I consider pinching him just to make sure he's real

love leaks from my heart till every fiber of my being
throbs with a warmth, so natural and freeing

I've never cared much for love stories or any cheesy line
yet here I am adoring him and forcing words to rhyme.

Such is love.

Malika Kahn is a South African writer, editor, and lifelong learner with a penchant for reading multiple books at once. She lives in Cape Town with her wonderful family and imaginary cats.

Dylan Webster

DYAD

The doubt of continuance
Like the shadow of pride
Haunts you through all halls
Down which you walk
Draping you like a shroud --
A dyad mutually feeding
And mutually drawing
All of your blood.

Hegemony

Speak clearly
and think soberly
and act properly
in accordance
with
my speech
my thought
my action.
Hegemonic
I am your master
your lover
your logic
your life.

I AM NOT MY OWN

Softened, heated lips brand my skin
Sealing me with marks of your heart
The burning of your passion,
The tensing of your body
Speaking in a language only felt
Communicating what burns in the blood,
Displayed as art above me --
& in your eyes i saw the change
The metamorphosis, you ascending,
Spirit soaring, while your body writhes mine
Into submission, my voice mute with passion,
Our union has created a new form,
And you tense your body
To claim me as your own,
Taking me and holding me within
Like the most precious gift
Hid from prying eyes,
And finally your lungs sing the praise
Your body exuded, in a breathless
Yet heavy singing exhale
And sharp inhale,
Like the rising and
Descent on me
Until you draw
All of me
Onto you.

Dylan Webster lives and writes in the sweltering heat of Phoenix, AZ with his wife and son. His poetry and fiction can be found in Quillkeepers' Press Anthologies, The Dillydoun Review, and Cannons Mouth Quarterly. His debut collection of poetry – *Dislocated* - has recently been published by Quillkeeper's Press.

Sophia Turner

The Tower

Is it normal to choke on the words you
can't say

Or give your hand to fate and make *him* lead the way

Because I am too afraid to be my own demise

But I have too much pride to give into your eyes

So meet me halfway

Or build the whole bridge

As I squint from the tower to see what this is

The Ballroom

She gives him one dance

Though her heart's in a trance
Her dreams still remember the brush of his hands

Cause his eyes wouldn't change
Though beauty would fade

Her lips cried to taste

The strength of his name

She swayed in the ballroom
Though darkness it called him

He gritted his teeth he defended their honor

She gave him one dance
Though her heart's in a trance and
Her dreams still remember the brush of his hands

Cause her eyes wouldn't change
Though beauty would fade

Her lips never taste
His strong embrace
Or the honor of sharing the strength of his name

The Hope

Know that hidden behind my eyes was everything I'd miss
And the violent longing you'd remember the day we almost
kissed

In hope or in fear
Of all I didn't say

In both daydreams and nightmares
I whisper your name

The Longing

I grit my teeth and I thrash
and I rage
I scream and I mumble and I choke your name

I tell you I'm sorry
Cause
I said I'd be strong

But your life was the very thing I learned to long

So I whisper I'm sorry
Cause
I know I'm not strong

But your breath was the cadence to
all of my songs

So I'll cry and I'll scream and I'll mumble your name
If it lowers me closer to the edge of your grave

The Rage

F*** you hero because I am your bride

My sanity's chained to the sways of your tide

It thrashes away when you phase in my mind
I picked out their names and I prayed and I tried

But you threw it away the day that you died
Now the tales of your glory are my heart's demise

And your silence it screams in the depths of my eyes

Sophia Turner is a poet and literary enthusiast. She lives in Florida with her seven siblings, severe caffeine addiction, and brooding, but adorable, white pitbull.

David Greshel

A Waltz Unremembered

It's a weird thing
The ghosts we chase
The phantoms we attempt to resurrect
On the assumption this life is better
Than where their journey has taken them
A kind of empathetic selfishness
Born in the throes of grief

It's not that we want to keep them here
In the midst of their suffering
Or that we ascribe ourselves in deity
We just want an alternative experience
One that doesn't involve such pain
Or such an early exit

That's the mystery though, isn't it?
The unseen gamble of the living
Banking on aces and eights
We always want more time at the end
When there was so much story
To live along the way

I just want one more dance with you
One more day in the light
One last chance to tell you
All of the 'I love yous'
I never got to say

Hopelessly Devoted Rushing In

I played the jester once
Though I much prefer the bard
Dealing in flashes of brilliance
And an adventure in song
To the fire eating juggler
With a joke and a rhyme

Yes, I played the fool
How could I not?

We were always on this path
Star-crossed and predestined
Bound for the yellowed pages
Of a 'stranger than fiction' tell-all
And the movie of the week

Despite the looming futility
I went to war and bled for you
Sacrificed my prime
And in my pain I promised you tomorrow
Like I spoke for days and seasons

Yes, I am a fool
The question is... whose?

'Looking Back on Today' was Never our Song

Skyward sonatas serenade in solitude
The drifting voices finding harmony
In equal parts aligned in rhyme
That lend themselves to meditation
And other subtle attempts
To soothe more savage reactions

Really, what more could I have done?
I've replayed the scenarios a thousand times
Looking for answers that don't exist
Or pages I might've missed
To explain the current outcome
And this gnawing hole in my chest

'I painted your name on my bones'
Knit you into my inner being
To keep your ghost contained
Bound our souls to a fading memory
That last number on our jukebox
And the comfort of a fallen night

The Music's Never Over and our Light is Eternal

I've often wondered at length
If you think I don't remember
All the moments we've captured
The inseparable nature
Of entire summers spent entwined
Or the burning brilliant inferno
Encased in our winter embrace

In what world would I ever forget you?
The touch of your slender tips
Gliding across my skin
Like fingered strings on a violin
Lingering in the perfect time

No, I remember every one
Flickering on the home movie memory reel
Reciting them back
In the lines of our favorite films
Writing this poem of us
On the flesh of our pounding hearts
And in the breath of this unending kiss

Last Stop 'til Thunderdome

"I just can't anymore"
Words that leave a hollow sound
And a hint of death on the tongue
Percolating in the steaming morass
Of what we never quite achieved
Only sort of believed
But still held out for the hope
Floating with messages in bottles
To illuminate our shared experience

Of course, that was before
We tripped over the weight of ego
And ran out of the slightest evens
Settled in the dust of remember whens
Built on the backs of never again
And the whispers of might've been

Exhausting
That's the simplest descriptor
And the truest
(if honesty is what we're aiming for)
This dance we've found ourselves in
Tiresome and repetitive
A pugilistic pantomime
Undersold and overhyped
And I'm tired...so tired...

At least let me dream it the way it's meant to be

Lakeview Municipal Route 36

The sunlight creeps through the spaces between the towering high-rises that punctuate the thriving urban landscape. Alternating slashes of liquid gold and indigo shadows fall across the early morning rush hour as the downtown metropolis shakes off its slumber and teems with throngs of thousands scrambling into their routines for work or school, filling the network of concrete and asphalt arteries with all manner of cars, trucks, bicycles, skateboards, and busses. Electric lights flickered on in storefronts all along the avenues, beckoning to passersby with promises of caffeine and pastry and an assortment of other championship breakfast offerings. In between orders for double espresso shots and bear claws the air is filled with the unmistakable cacophony of an automobile symphony, played on impatient horns and rattling engines accented by colorful phrases bellowed in fits of anger. It was exhilarating, maybe even a bit unnerving, for the uninitiated urban acolyte.

Danny loved mornings here in the city. Each one was full of the promise of something new and unique to experience on his bus route through downtown and out to the art district. He had been a driver for the city of Lakeview for the last 30 years, and a lifelong resident. He had watched it grow from the sleepy little village of his childhood into a shining beacon of a modern urban landscape. It felt like it happened so fast, but he didn't mind the change. By his reckoning, the whole world was changing at a pace he could only just barely keep up with. That was alright, though, he had his own morning routine that he kept to and it suited him just fine. He caught the 5:15 morning train into the city center and walked the six blocks to the bus depot to pick up Lizzy. He always made a quick stop at Mario's café for cup of dark roast and a pastry to tide him over until lunch. It was simple but he loved the uniformity of it, as it kept him on track and made his internal OCD scheduler happy.

"Mornin' Danny." Art never failed to greet him as he made his way into the depot. He was finishing up his late-night shift and waiting on the AM replacement to arrive. "G'mornin' Art. Hope it was a quiet evening for ya." This response always amused Art, or at least seemed to since he shot back a smile and replied, "Oh, it was just me and the strays, and they're not much interested in the busses." Danny laughed and made his way through the columns of vehicles until he came to Lizzy. She sat in the darkness of the back lot, illuminated by a single lamp. It always reminded Danny of a performer onstage lit up by the spotlight, ready for their big number. He took a handkerchief from his pocket and began gently polishing one of the headlights and front bumpers. "G'mornin' pretty lady. What's say you and me go for a drive today?" He had been driving this same bus for most of his career, and like any good captain he gave his ship a name. She wasn't new, but she was reliable and comfortable and he couldn't imagine driving another one. There had been many offers to let him move up to one of the newer models but he loved Lizzy too much to even consider doing so, and his tenure with the company still meant something to the current management so they didn't push the issue. "you've got too much life left in ya to stop now." He pulled himself up into the driver's seat and stroked his fingertips along the console fondly before pushing the buttons to start the engine. The crank sputtered slightly and then caught and hummed in time, purring and ready to challenge another day of stop and go traffic. "That's my girl. Let's go help some people get on their way." He smiled and did his final check before heading out of the depot and on to the first stop.

Chuck was already feeling out of sorts after ignoring his alarm for an hour. He wasn't quite sure what was bothering him, but he knew that another long day sitting in his cubicle at the brokerage was not going to improve his mood. Despite that, his bills were not going to just disappear so he quietly rebelled by tossing and turning while the alarm clock on the bedside table screeched and howled until he could no longer avoid recognizing the futility of this action. Great. And what's the result of this brilliant plan? A mad dash to shower, dress, and get breakfast down before he missed the 8:15 bus outside his apartment building. The bus wasn't always his first choice, but it was too late to make the walk and he refused to pay for a cab or an Uber. The bus travel was usually uneventful, and it usually meant that he could see Amy if he timed it right. She worked as a barista in the small coffee shop around the corner from his office, and Chuck had something of a crush on her. Who was he kidding, he had a major crush on her and he thought it must be painfully obvious to everyone. Amy didn't seem to notice, or if she did she was not about to let on. In his head, he had all these daydreams about the two of them and it was all very saccharine and Hollywood but he wasn't so naïve as to think that anything like that would happen. They had exchanged pleasantries in the past, and had a few mutual friends so they had been at a few dinner parties together, but he could never quite get up the nerve to ask her out on an actual date. He was a fairly successful analyst and dealt with high pressure situations on the regular, but walking over to her to have a conversation that would result in a question about a night out required a strength of will that he did not seem to possess. It would be comical if it wasn't so sad.

Chuck exited his building just in time to see the bus pull up and open the doors. "Well at least this part of the morning is going right," he thought to himself. He scanned his bus pass though the reader and made his way to an empty seat. Still caught up in his muddled thoughts from earlier this morning, he didn't notice until he sat down that Amy was sitting across the aisle from him. It was a slightly chilly morning, so she had on a coat and a scarf with her long red hair cascading down to her shoulders. Her green eyes had a bit of a gleam in the morning sun and she was trying to focus on the book in her hands. God, she was so beautiful and Chuck just wanted to take her by the hand and profess his undying love for her and promise to carry her off into the sunset into a life she'd always dreamed of. They would be happy and carefree and take afternoon picnics at the beach, with long walks and sunsets and....and damn it he was dreaming again.

"Hi Chuck." The sound of her voice snapped him back to reality. She had looked up from her book and smiled at him. He smiled back a bit sheepishly, "hey Amy. Nice morning, huh? Are you ready for another day in paradise?" "Oh, if this is paradise then someone owes me a refund. I'm looking at you Eddie Money." They both laughed at her joke and then she went back to reading while He fumbled over all the things he wanted to say. It was fairly typical of their recent interactions and Chuck was wondering if this would be it. Time felt like it was crawling in these moments, and in his slightly off-kilter feeling today he actually called out to the driver, "Hey man, can we pick up the pace a bit? I don't want to miss my first meeting." That wasn't at all true, Chuck hated all of the morning meetings and virtually everyone would be better served as an email that he could ignore.

"Keep your shirt on boyo, Lizzy and I will get you there on time, don't you worry," The driver called back cheerily. "Oooookkkk" Chuck wondered who Lizzy was but already felt a bit bad for being snippy with him so he decided to ignore it. "Everything alright Chuck? That was odd for you…" Amy was eyeing him but with a look of actual concern that he hadn't seen before. "Yeah, I'm ok I'm just a little bit off today and I can't quite put my finger on why." He paused for a moment, trying to compose his thoughts. "Hey Amy, I was actually wondering…" The bus came to a stop and the driver announced, "5th and Queens." "Oh hey, that's us. What were you saying Chuck?" Amy was standing up and gathering her things and getting ready to move into the aisle. "It's nothing really, I'll see you later on for a lunchtime caffeine buzz?" She smiled and headed toward the front of the bus, "You know where I'll be. Have a good day!" "You too." He stood up and shuffled to the front, pausing when he got to the driver. "I'm sorry I was snippy with you earlier sir. I've just got a lot on my mind I guess." The driver smiled at him sympathetically. "Don't worry about it son, it takes a lot more than that to get me riled up. Do you mind if I offer you some advice?" Chuck looked at him quizzically, "Uh, sure…" The driver leaned a bit closer. "I couldn't help but notice that you fancy the young lady that was sitting across from you and it looked like you were trying to screw up the nerve to ask her something…" Chuck was starting to turn a few shades darker. "It's nothing to be ashamed of, and I imagine we've all stumbled about trying to find the best words to woo the women we've fallen in love with…" Christ, did this guy drop out of Shakespeare? "…and all I'm trying to say is don't wait. Life is too short and there's too much of it to spend alone. If you like her, then tell her." He smiled again and Chuck stumbled through tactfully exiting the awkward conversation. "Uh, yeah ok. Thanks for the tips old man." He stepped off of the bus and hurried up the street to the brokerage.

Danny chuckled to himself as he watched the young man go. "Lizzy wasn't I just as tongue tied with you?" He patted the dashboard and smiled. The rest of the day was uneventful and he made his way back to the depot. He parked in the waiting spot and made his round through the bus. Collecting trash and items for the lost and found box in the office. "Another good day old girl, let's have another go tomorrow." He pulled the door shut and head out of the depot to catch the evening train.

Later that night, as he was pulling himself into bed, he thought about the young couple on the bus. It all seemed so familiar and it brought back a flood of memories. He was young and shy once too, and he met the most beautiful girl that made his stomach do somersaults any time she came near. The most beautiful, most patient girl who waited for him to finally develop some stones and ask her to the dance. They were inseparable from that moment, and it was a magical life.
"It was another good day Lizzy..." he kissed his fingertips and brushed them over the picture on the nightstand. "Let's have another go tomorrow." With that, he turned off the lamp and rolled on his side with his arm draped over the empty spot beside him.

David Greshel is a Mississippi-born, Florida-bred author and poet with a penchant for music, movies, and all things pop culture. Never one to shy away from self-reflection and evaluation, he channels it all into his writing with the results you now see before you.

David currently resides in Palm Bay Florida and can often be found at live music events when not working, writing, or spending time with friends and family.

David has four poetry collections — Postcards from a City Ablaze, Windows into the Past for the Camera Shy, Nomads, Pilgrims, Troubadours, and Fallen Sky, Bought and Sold — that are available everywhere.

Connect with David:

Email: dgreshel217@gmail.com
Facebook: facebook.com/david.greshel
Instagram: @electricinfamy
Twitter: @electricinfamy
Website: www.neonsunrisebooks.com

Other Anthologies available from
Neon Sunrise Publishing:

MEMOIRS OF A BROKEN PEOPLE

A LIGHT THAT
NEVER GOES OUT

A Neon Sunrise Anthology

Dead Signals//
Lost Transmissions

A Neon Sunrise Anthology

Neon Sunrise Publishing is focused on helping independent creators realize their dreams of seeing their books in print. We're driven by a DIY spirit and a desire to provide options and resources to help developing talent succeed in sharing their voice with the world.

To keep up with all of our latest news and releases, be sure to join our mailing list and connect with us online!

Email:	neonsunrisepub@gmail.com
Facebook:	facebook.com/neonsunrisepub
Instagram:	@neonsunrisepub
Twitter:	@neonsunrisepub
Website:	www.neonsunrisepublishing.com